CONTENTS
Stories

The Stolen Ring . . . . Proverbs 28:11 4

Better Than the Beach . . . . Hebrews 10:25 9

A Wasted Birthday Present? . . . . . .Psalm 122:1 13

The Robber's Revenge . . . . Habakkuk 2:20 18

Mother Doesn't Love Us Anymore Proverbs 3:5 22

Island Prisoner, Part I . . . . Matthew 6:24 26

Island Prisoner, Part II . . . . Isaiah 34:16 32

Island Prisoner, Part III . . . . .Psalm 119:11 38

The Broken Window . . . . James 1:22 44

That Old Red Sweater . . . . James 1:22 48

Gulab and the Tiger Hunt . . . . .Revelation 22:12 52

Nellie's Reward . . . . Revelation 22:12 56

Songs

Even a Child 8

I Was Glad 12

The Lord is in His Holy Temple 21

Trusting Jesus 59

Give of Your Best to the Master 60

Read Your Bible 17

Thy Word Have I Hid in My Heart 61

Jesus Christ is Coming for Me 51

Appendix

Suggested Plan for One Quarter's Assembly Period 62

Suggested Program for the End of the Quarter 63

Scripture Catechism Card, "Conduct Toward God" 64

THE STOLEN RING

**"Even a child is known by his doings; whether his work
be pure, and whether it be right." Proverbs 20:11**

"I like Carla Anderson best of all my friends," Julie Jones announced at dinner.

"Why?" asked her mother.

"Carla always plays what I want to play," said Julie. "The other girls only want to play what they want to play."

Father laughed. "You like this girl because she helps to spoil you."

But Julie's mother did not laugh. She said, "Isn't Carla the welfare child who steals?"

"Carla used to take things," said Julie, "but she goes to Sunday School with me, so she doesn't do that any more."

"I don't see how going to Sunday School would make all that difference," said Julie's father soberly.

Julie said, "It's not just going to Sunday School. Carla has let the Lord Jesus into her heart."

Dinner was over and no one said any more about Carla.

The next afternoon Carla came home from school with Julie as she had often done lately. Although they were fourth graders both girls still liked to play with dolls. This afternoon they washed all the doll clothes out on the back porch. Then they went into the house to play for a while.

Carla was about to go home when Julie suddenly exclaimed, "Where's my ring?"

"I don't know," said Carla. "Maybe you didn't have it on today."

"Yes, I did," said Julie. "Oh now I remember. I took it off when we washed the doll clothes. I set it on the porch railing."

Julie rushed out to the porch to get her ring and Carla followed. But it was not there.

"Maybe it fell down below," suggested Carla. Both girls looked all over the ground and all over the porch but they could not find the ring.

Julie's mother came out and asked "What are you girls looking for?"

"For my ring," said Julie.

"I hope you haven't lost the gold ring Grandmother gave you," exclaimed her mother.

"Yes," said Julie. "I can't find it anywhere."

"When did you have it last?" asked her mother.

"I took it off to wash the doll clothes," said Julie. "I set it here on the porch railing. But when I came to look for it, it was gone."

"You should never have set it down like that," said her mother. "I have told you time and again that whenever you take it off you must put it in the box on your dresser." Then Mrs. Jones looked at Carla, "Maybe your friend knows where your ring is."

"No, I don't," said Carla, but her face got red.

Julie looked at Carla. She remembered that when one of the girls had lost her big new box of crayolas it was found in Carla's desk. And another time when a boy had lost a quarter, it was found in Carla's pocket.

"Did you take my ring?" asked Julie, looking straight at her friend.

"No," said Carla looking ready to cry.

"Where is it then?" asked Julie's mother.

"I don't know," said Carla miserably. "Maybe someone else took it."

"No one else has been here," said Julie's mother coldly. "It's time for you to go home now and I don't want you to come back here again till Julie's ring is found."

The next day at school the other girls noticed that Julie would not speak to Carla. They asked Julie what had happened. She said, "Carla stole my gold ring."

Miss Martin, the fourth grade teacher noticed that Carla looked very sad and that none of the other girls spoke to her. Miss Martin was a Christian and taught Junior girls in Sunday School. Both Julie and Carla were in that class.

Miss Martin knew that Julie and Carla had been best friends so she asked Julie to stay in the room for a minute at lunch time. She smiled at Julie when she asked her this, so the rest of the class knew it was not a punishment.

Miss Martin asked Julie, "Do you know what is the matter with Carla?"

"Yes," said Julie. "She stole my gold ring so I won't be friends with her anymore."

"Are you sure Carla stole your ring?" asked Miss Martin.

"Yes," said Julie. Then she told Miss Martin all about it. Miss Martin asked, "Did you tell the other girls about this?"

"Yes," said Julie.

"I'm sorry you did that," said Miss Martin. "The Bible says, 'Speak not evil one of another.' That means that we should never tell anything bad about another person except to someone who might be able to help. Sometimes it is right to tell about someone else's wrong doing to your parents or to your teacher or even to a policeman, but it is never right to tell such things to everyone." Then Miss Martin added, "I will talk to Carla about it."

No one spoke to Carla all that next day except the teacher. Just before school was out she asked Carla to stay after school a minute.

As soon as the other children had gone, Miss Martin sat down beside Carla and put her arm around her. She said, "Did you really mean it the day you asked the Lord Jesus to come into your heart and take your sins away?"

"Yes," said Carla.

"I'm so glad," said her teacher. "But did you know that even after we are saved, we are sometimes tempted to do wrong?"

"Yes," said Carla again.

Miss Martin said, "If we yield to the temptation and do wrong, we cannot be happy until we have confessed that sin. The Bible says, 'If we confess our sins, He is faithful and just to forgive us our sins and to cleanse us from all unrighteousness.' If you took Julie's ring, you have two things to do to be right with the Lord. You must give the ring back to Julie and confess your sin to the Lord."

"But I didn't take Julie's ring," said Carla crying.

Miss Martin said "The Lord knows all about it. He hears every word we say. You know that, don't you Carla?"

"Yes," sobbed Carla.

"Does the Lord know that you did not take Julie's ring?" asked her teacher.

"Yes," said Carla again.

"I believe you," said Miss Martin, putting both arms around her.

The next morning Miss Martin said to the class, "I do not believe that Carla stole Julie's ring. And I don't want you to treat her as if she were a thief."

One child asked, "Who could have taken it then?"

"I do not know," said the teacher, "but I am sure Carla did not take it."

Some of the girls spoke to Carla after that, but not Julie. She said to the other girls, "Miss Martin is just sorry for Carla because she is a welfare child. But I think it was awfully mean of her to steal my ring when we were best friends."

Carla knew that her teacher believed in her and most of the children were polite to her but she knew that many of them believed that she was still a thief. How Carla wished that she had never taken something that did not belong to her! She realized that was what made everyone so ready to believe that she was still a thief.

One afternoon several weeks later Julie's brother Bob and one of his friends were playing ball in the back yard. Julie asked if she could play too. The boys reluctantly agreed. When it was Julie's turn to bat the ball, she hit it in such a way it went up into a tree. And it did not come down. "Just like a girl," jeered Bob as he climbed the tree to look for the ball.

In a short time he called out, "You'd never guess where the ball went. You couldn't have batted it in here if you had tried. It's in that old blue jay's nest. I'm going to bring it down to show you."

Bob brought down the blue jay's nest containing the ball. It was amazing that the ball had fallen into it, for it was a tight fit.

But when Bob succeeded in getting the ball out, Julie uttered an exclamation, "My gold ring!" Sure enough, there it was. One of the blue jays must have seen it the day that Julie laid it on the porch railing. For some reason the bird had taken it to its nest.

Just then Julie saw Miss Martin going past. She ran out to the front of the house and called, "Miss Martin, a blue jay stole my ring, not Carla."

Miss Martin came to look at the nest with the ring in it. "What are you going to do about this?" she asked Julie.

"If Mother will let me, I will phone Carla and ask her to come to supper. I want to tell her how sorry I am and I want to show her the ring before I take it out of the nest."

Julie's mother said, "Yes, do invite Carla. We have been unfair to her." Then Mrs. Jones said to Miss Martin, "Won't you stay for supper too?"

Carla arrived at Julie's house looking puzzled. She was glad that Julie had invited her again but she couldn't think what had happened. Julie hugged Carla as soon as she got there. She said, "I'm dreadfully sorry that I said you stole my ring. I thought you had because I couldn't think of anywhere else it could be. I was very wrong to tell the other girls that you had stolen it. Will you forgive me and be my best friend again?"

"Of course I will," said Carla nearly crying for joy. I can't blame you for thinking I stole it because it disappeared and I used to be a thief. But I'm not one now because I belong to Jesus."

Miss Martin reminded the girls of one of their memory verses, "Even a child is known by his doings, whether his work be pure and whether it be right." Then she said, "Once Carla had the reputation of being a thief, but now she is building the reputation of being a good, honest, Christian girl. People do notice how children behave and it is important to build a good reputation. But never forget that God also notices how we behave and what He thinks is most important of all."

Even a Child

Barbara Ryberg

Dorothy L. Braun

8

BETTER THAN THE BEACH

A true story of people known to the writer

**"Not forsaking the assembling of ourselves together,
as the manner of some is." Hebrews 10:25**

Dickie Duncan was only seven years old, but every morning as soon as breakfast was over he ran outside to play with the other boys in the neighborhood. Sometimes they played in the near-by woods, more often they would play ball on the school grounds a little way up the road. All summer long Dickie played outdoors, but the greatest treat of the summer was when his folks took him to the beach! He loved to run on the smooth sand. He hunted for pretty shells. He made castles in the sand. He paddled in the water and tried to swim. Dickie wished he could go to the beach every day, but since it was many miles away, he only got to go three or four times in the whole summer.

One bright morning, a young lady, Miss Dorothy, called at Dickie's home. She told his mother that she was going to have a Vacation Bible School in the community, and asked her if she would be willing for her children to come. Mrs. Duncan answered:

"My girl might have gone, but she is away spending a couple of weeks with her grandmother. I'm sure my boy wouldn't care to go. Dickie just loves the outdoors. I never see him from morning till night all summer."

Miss Dorothy said: "We are going to have story time outdoors under the trees, if it stays as nice as it is now. Are you willing for Dickie to come if he wants to?"

"It's alright with me if he wants to," said Mrs. Duncan, "but I don't think he'll stay long. He's always on the go."

Miss Dorothy went to the school grounds where the boys were playing. "I'm going to be out here for a few days," she said pleasantly, "and I know some good stories. Would you like to sit down in the shade and listen to one?" The boys were hot and tired, so after exchanging looks which meant, "If we don't like it, we can run off," they sat down. Miss Dorothy told them about three boys thrown into a burning, fiery furnace, and then she invited them to Bible School the next day to hear another story. She said, "If the sun is shining we will have the story out under the trees." The boys, including Dickie, decided to come.

Dickie and his friends came to Bible School every morning, and for the first time in his life Dickie heard the story of the Lord Jesus. One morning Miss Dorothy said, "If any of you children would like to take the Lord Jesus as your Saviour, stay a few minutes after the rest go, so I can be sure you understand what it means." Dickie stayed. That day he asked the Saviour to come into his heart, and to wash away all his sins. He went home happier than he had ever been before in his short life.

Before the Bible School ended, Miss Dorothy taught the children the Bible verse which says, "Not forsaking the assembling of ourselves together, as the manner of some is" (Heb. 10:25). She said: "The Lord Jesus does not want you to forget Him as soon as Bible School is ended. Some children forget Him and stop coming to learn about Him and that makes Him sad. He died on the cross so that you might go to Heaven. Do not disappoint Him. Go to Sunday school *every Sunday* to learn more about Him."

Dickie, and the other children who had been saved, started to go to Sunday school and learned more and more about Jesus. And Dickie tried to please his Saviour by being more helpful and obedient at home. He came to Sunday school every Sunday, even though no one else in his family was interested in the things of the Lord.

One evening at suppertime, Dickie's father said, "How would you like to go to the beach tomorrow?"

"Oh, can we!" exclaimed Dickie. "Hurray, hurray," and he almost jumped up from the table in his excitement. That evening Dickie got out his swimming trunks, his toy boat, his sand pail and shovel, and he could think of nothing else but the wonderful trip to the beach the next day.

The next morning they were off early, just stopping long enough to pick up Dickie's aunt and cousins who lived a few miles nearer to the water. The uncle had to work, but said he would come out to the beach as soon as he got done and would stay until they came home. The children talked happily about all the fun they would have at the beach, and at last they were there. With a whoop of delight Dickie and his cousins raced across the sand. They had been told not to go swimming till later in the day, but they could dig in the sand, wade, and run along the beach. After a while the cousins decided to make a castle. Dickie went back to the car to get his shovel and pail. He heard his aunt say, "I wish we could manage to come a different day than Sunday—the beach gets so crowded as the day goes on."

Sunday! Dickie had never once realized that this was Sunday! Why, he should be at home in Sunday school!

Dickie went over to his father. "I didn't know this was Sunday," he said; "I must go to Sunday school!"

"Not today," said Mr. Duncan. "You can go *next* Sunday, if you want to."

"But the Lord Jesus wants us to go *every* Sunday," said Dickie earnestly. "I must go today, too."

"Don't be ridiculous," said his father. "Your Sunday school is more than thirty miles away. It is impossible for you to go today. Run away and play."

But Dickie did not go. He started to cry. "The Lord Jesus wants me to go to Sunday school *today*. He died for me. I don't want to disappoint Him."

His father stared at him. Then he remembered how much better Dickie had behaved since he started talking about the Lord Jesus. "It really means something to him," he thought.

Dickie was crying in good earnest now. "For goodness' sake," said Dickie's aunt, "if any of my kids were that crazy about Sunday school, I'd sure take them! I think Sunday school is good for kids, but mine don't care too much about it."

"Look here, Dick," said his father. "If I take you back to Sunday school, we don't come back to the beach today—understand?"

"Yes," said Dickie.

"Would you really rather go back to Sunday school and miss the whole day at the beach? Think twice before you answer, because most likely we won't come out again this summer."

"I would rather go to Sunday school," said Dick, "because I don't want to disappoint the Lord Jesus."

Mr. Duncan looked at his wife, "It looks as if you'll have to take him home," said Mrs. Duncan. "But Mollie won't want to go."

"Oh, you and Mollie stay here," said the aunt quickly. "We mustn't spoil the day for the other kids. My husband will gladly run you home when he takes us."

So Dickie went back home with his father. He hated to miss a day at the beach because he thought that was the best fun in the world, but he loved the Lord Jesus more.

Although Dickie's Sunday school did not start till eleven o'clock, he was a little late, but he smiled all over as he said to his teacher, "I was out at the beach, but I remembered that verse, 'Not forsaking the assembling of ourselves together, as the manner of some is,' and I finally got here."

Mr. Duncan could not forget that his little boy had chosen Sunday school instead of a day at the beach. He decided to go to church himself to see what it was all about. Dickie's mother and sister went, too.

When Miss Dorothy came back the next summer Dickie said, "I didn't forget about the Lord Jesus. I go to Sunday school *every* Sunday. Now everybody at our house loves the Lord Jesus."

Dickie's Sunday school teacher told Miss Dorothy the story I have just told you. She said, "So Dickie helped all his family to get saved because he loves the Lord Jesus better than the beach."

Reprinted by permission of "The Sunday School Times"

I Was Glad

Copyright, 1943, by Scripture Press. Used by permission.

After this song is familiar, three children may each sing one of the three repeated phrases, and all may sing, "Let us go into the house of the Lord."

12

A WASTED BIRTHDAY PRESENT?

**"I was glad when they said unto me, Let us go into
the house of the Lord." Psalm 122:1**

"Can't we have Sunday School any more?" Jack Durant asked his Sunday School teacher anxiously. It was Thanksgiving Day and Jack's birthday, so the widowed Mrs. Morrell had asked Jack to dinner. She knew that his father paid no attention to birthdays or holidays so that Jack would miss his mother even more at such a time.

Now that they had finished eating, Mrs. Morrell had told Jack that she had received notice to move from the house she had lived in for the last twenty years. It had been sold and the new owner planned to tear it down and build a more modern house there.

Mrs. Morrell was the only active Christian worker in the little community. Once a month a preacher came to speak in the little church. But Mrs. Morrell was there every week conducting a Sunday School for any who cared to come. Jack's mother taught a class there but she had now been in heaven for several months. Jack had come to know the Lord in that little Sunday School and he loved that morning hour more than any other time in the week.

There were no vacant houses in the district so now Mrs. Morrell would have to go and live somewhere among strangers. Jack felt sorry for her and besides he wondered what he would do without her and without his weekly time in the house of the Lord.

When Jack went home from the Thanksgiving dinner he prayed that the Sunday School might not close and also that his friend the Sunday School teacher might not have to move far away.

Jack thought about Mrs. Morrell many times that day. He thought about the man who had bought her house. Maybe the man didn't know that she had rented it for so many years. Maybe he didn't know about the Sunday School. Would it make any difference to him if he did?

Friday was a pouring wet day. After Jack's father had gone to work, Jack did a few things around the house. Then he stood looking out the window and almost wished it was not a holiday. He saw the mailman driving down the road. To his surprise the man stopped and put something into their mailbox. This only happened when it was time for some bill even though bills usually came at the very end of the month or at the beginning of the next one. However he dashed out in the rain to see.

The envelope was addressed to him. It was from his uncle who lived hundreds of miles away. When Jack opened it he found that it held a birthday card containing a five dollar bill. His uncle had written on the card: "Your twelfth birthday is an important date. Your aunt and I wanted to send you something but since we don't know what you would like, we are sending you the money to spend any way you wish."

Jack was surprised and delighted. He had not seen his uncle and aunt since his mother's funeral and he had not heard from them either. He did not remember them ever having sent him a present before and he had never had as much as five dollars to spend as he pleased.

Jack thought about getting a new fishing pole or some accessories for his bicycle. Should he spend his money in the little country store or should he wait till his father went to the city? Jack did not know when his father might go. Maybe before Christmas, maybe after. His father would not go till he wanted something he could not get locally.

Jack's thoughts went back to Mrs. Morrell and her trouble. Suddenly he had an idea. Perhaps if he could see the man who had bought her place and tell him about the Sunday School he might change his mind about tearing her house down.

At suppertime Jack showed his father the card and birthday present. Then he asked him if he could go to the city the next day. His father said, "Well, now that you are twelve years old I suppose you are old enough to go alone on the bus if you are sure that is the way you want to spend your money. But you must get back before dark." Then he added, "Be sure you don't get lost."

Next morning Jack hurried over to Mrs. Morrell's house. He told her about his birthday present and his plan to find the man who had bought her place. She said, "That's a very kind thought, Jack, but don't bother about me. You might have trouble finding his address and if you did find it he might not be home or he might not listen to you."

"I want to try," said Jack. "Please let me copy his address off the letter you got."

Mrs. Morrell reluctantly let him copy the address but she said, "Don't get lost looking for his place and don't be disappointed if he isn't home or won't listen to you." Then she said "I may have to move but I believe the Lord will keep the Sunday School going in some way. I hope you have a pleasant day and that you find something you would like to have in one of the stores there."

Jack enjoyed the bus ride. And when he got to the city he looked at the Christmas decorations and glanced at one or two store windows. Then he decided that he had better find the man first and after that go into the stores.

He showed the address to a policeman, and asked him how to get there. The policeman said, "That's a good way out of the city. You'll have to take a city bus to get there, and then walk from the end of the line. You can ask your way at the little store where the bus turns around."

Jack thanked the policeman and then stood on the street corner waiting for the bus. He realized that after he paid this bus fare he would not have much money to spend in the stores. Jack had to wait quite a while for the right bus but at last it came.

When Jack got on this bus he thought he would soon be at his destination but it made so many stops that this trip took him almost as long as it had taken him to get from his home to the city. As he rode along he prayed silently that the Lord would make the man be at home and would make him listen to him.

At last the bus reached the end of its route. When Jack asked at the store for directions to the man's house, it proved to be quite a long walk to get there. Jack liked to walk but just now he felt impatient because he realized that he would have to walk back to the bus afterward and the day was going by.

When Jack finally arrived at the right address he had to walk quite a distance along a winding driveway. Then he reached the house. It proved to be such a grand house he was almost afraid to go up to the door to ring the bell.

As he stood there a man came around the house. He asked Jack what he wanted. Jack said he wanted to see Mr. Brownley. The man said, "Too bad. You can't see him today because he left just a few minutes ago and said he would not be back till night."

Jack was bitterly disappointed. He had spent most of his money to make this trip and it had proved to be useless after all. There was nothing to do but walk back to the place where he could catch the bus. When he got there he found that he would have to wait about an hour. By this time he was really hungry. He realized too that he would have to take the bus for home almost as soon as he reached the city. Otherwise he would not get home before dark. So he decided to spend the rest of his birthday present for some food.

Jack was right. When he got back to the city there was no time to look around the stores. The bus to his home would leave in ten minutes. His money was gone anyway, so he went to the bus depot. While Jack was waiting for the bus to take him home he felt more disappointed than he had ever been in his life.

A man also waiting for the bus looked at Jack's sad face. He said, "Are you tired, my boy?"

"Yes," said Jack "but I don't mind that. I'm just so disappointed to have come to the city all for nothing."

"What did you come for?" asked the man kindly.

"I came to talk to a man about a house," said Jack.

"That sounds interesting," said the man. "Suppose we sit together on the bus and you tell me about it."

"Most boys don't come to the city to talk to a man about a house," said the stranger after they were seated. "So I would like to know more about your errand." Then Jack told his new friend all about Mrs. Morrell and the Sunday School. He told him how hard it would be for her to have to move to a new place where she did not know anyone, and he told the man how much he wanted the Sunday School to continue. Since his new friend seemed so interested Jack told him about his five dollars and the long trip he had taken that day. He ended by saying "So you see I just wasted my birthday present."

"What is the name of the man you went to see?" asked the stranger. When Jack told him the man said, "I suppose you have now given up the hope of helping your friend."

"Well," said Jack sadly, "I don't have the money to go to the city again but I can still pray about it. God didn't answer my prayer today but Mother used to say that God answers prayer in His own way, and that we should trust Him. Mrs. Morrell says the same thing."

"Your mother and your Sunday School teacher are right," said the man. "But God did answer your prayer today."

"What do you mean?" asked Jack.

"I am Mr. Brownley," said his new friend. "The day I looked your Sunday School teacher's place over and decided to buy it, she was not at home. I decided to go back today to make more definite plans about building. I started out in my car but it developed a knock so I left it at a garage and came on by bus. I had more time to listen to your story on the bus than I would have had at home. I believe the Lord planned it all. I am going to see Mrs. Morrell now and I will tell her that my plans have changed. She can live in that house as long as she wants to. I shall also tell her to be sure to keep the Sunday School going."

"Oh, thank you! Thank you!" cried Jack. "Isn't that wonderful?"

When Jack got home his father asked what he had bought in the city, Jack said, "nothing."

"How much money have you left?" asked his father.

"None," said Jack.

"What makes you look so happy then?" asked his father.

Jack told him. His father said, "You really did a good day's work. But I think we must get the birthday present next Saturday. I'll take you to town and we'll find one."

"Oh thank you!" exclaimed Jack. "There's only one thing I would like better."

"Whatever can that be?" asked his father.

"If you would only go to Sunday School and church with me," said Jack.

"Maybe you'll get both your wishes," said his father.

READ YOUR BIBLE
Tune: Chorus of Count Your Blessings

THE ROBBER'S REVENGE

**"The Lord is in His holy temple; let all the earth keep
silence before Him." Habakkuk 2:20**

"When Policeman Correll arrested me, I told him that as soon
as I got out of jail, I'd make him sorry for the rest of his life," said
Alex Gomez to himself, "and I'm going to do it. Because of him I
had to spend five years in prison. During my first year I planned to
kill him, but now I have another plan. I'll kill his wife and little girl.
He'll suffer more that way."

Alex Gomez had talked to himself when alone in a prison cell
and so he did it now as he walked along the lonely road leading to
the state park where Bob Correll now lived. In summer the park was
full of people, but now that it was winter the place was deserted
except for the caretaker and his family.

Bob Correll had given up his police job soon after Alex Gomez
had been sentenced, and had become caretaker in this state park. As
soon as Gomez had gotten out of prison he had enquired for Bob
Correll. On his way to the state park he had learned that Correll was
away from home getting a new part for the water system which had
broken down. Since Bob Correll could not get home till the next
day, Gomez believed that fortune had given him the opportunity to
commit the crime he planned.

When he reached the Correll home it was beginning to get
dark. He fingered his knife as he looked over the place. Mrs. Correll
was taking clothes off the line behind the house. The little girl,
Amy, was running after her kitten. Gomez kept out of sight and
tried the front door. It was not locked so he slipped quietly inside
and hid in the closet under the staircase. "If they don't see me before, I'll wait till they are asleep in bed," he muttered. "After all,
it's not the fault of the kid or her mother. I'd like to kill them without their ever knowing what happened. I don't want to hurt them
but I want to spoil Correll's life; he spoiled mine."

Mrs. Correll and Amy soon came in and ate supper. After supper Amy said to her mother "I know my verse for Sunday School already. It says 'The Lord is in His holy temple, let all the earth keep
silence before Him." Habakkuk 2:20"

That's a wonderful verse said her mother. It reminds us how
great God is. He is greater than all the people in the world put together. So everyone should listen to Him."

"Does that mean everyone should read the Bible?" asked

Amy.

"Yes," said her mother. "If only everyone in the world would read the Bible and do what God says, this world would be like heaven."

"I wish Daddy would read the Bible," said Amy.

"I believe he will some day if we keep on praying for him," said Mrs. Correll. But now it is time for *us* to read the Bible.

Amy's mother read aloud the first part of Psalm 71 while Amy listened. Unknown to them the robber listened too. He had never heard such words before.

When Mrs. Correll stopped reading, Amy said "You read about a cruel man. Is that the man that wanted to hurt Father?"

"That Psalm was written before he was born," said her mother. But he must be a cruel man if he wants to hurt your father. Bob was only doing his duty when he arrested him."

"Will God take care of Father?" asked Amy.

"I pray that he will," said Mrs. Correll. "And I pray that your father may become a Christian. Then *he* could ask God to protect him. Now, Amy, it is time for us to pray. The two knelt down together. First Mrs. Correll prayed out loud, and then Amy. Amy prayed, "O God, please don't let the cruel man hurt Father. Please help him to listen to You and stop being cruel. Help Father to love you and help the cruel man to love you too."

Before long Amy and her mother went to bed. Soon the robber could tell that they were asleep. He came quietly out of the closet. A little moonlight came through the window. The robber held his knife in his hand and looked at Mrs. Correll and her little girl, both fast asleep. Then he looked at the table where the Bible lay still open. He tiptoed over to the table, set his knife down, and picked up the Bible. He tiptoed back to the front door. Mrs. Correll had locked the door but she had left the key in the lock. Gomez unlocked the door silently and went out taking the Bible with him.

Amy and her mother were both astonished and frightened when they got up the next morning and found the Bible missing and a knife on the table instead. When Amy's father came home he was surprised and alarmed. He realized that Gomez would probably be out of prison by that time so he got two good watch dogs. However nothing further alarming happened. Mrs. Correll got a new Bible and after a while the family almost forgot that strange occurence.

Carrying Correll's Bible the robber headed for a fishing village some miles distant. He had been a fisherman and decided to take up his trade again in a new place. Every day he read the Bible. He began to listen to God. The Bible showed him how bad he was. It also showed him that Christ died for his sins. One day he prayed to God. He said to Him, "I am a great sinner. I have been a thief and I had murder in my heart. But I believe Christ died for my sins and that He rose again. I want Him to save me from my sins and I want to belong to Him forever."

Not long after this, Alex Gomez married a fine Christian woman. He told her all about Bob Correll and his family. He said to her, "That policeman was pretty rough with me but then I fought him when he tried to arrest me. When I was in prison I blamed him for it but it was my own fault for stealing. And how I thank God for the Bible I took from Correll's home! I should return it to the family but they are not living in the same place now. If I hadn't heard what Amy and her mother said and then taken their Bible, I might have committed the terrible crime I planned and then I never never could have had a happy home of my own. And I'm sure that I would never have been happy again."

Mrs. Gomez said, "We can thank God for stopping you that night, and for making you into a changed man. I am sure that you will never steal again."

A few months later Bob Correll had business that took him past that fishing village. One of his front tires blew out and his car swerved into a tree. His car was badly damaged but he did not know it for he was knocked unconscious. Alex Gomez was the first one at the scene of the accident. There was no hospital in the village so Gomez took him into his own house and called the doctor. Before the doctor came Gomez realized that the injured man was his old enemy. The doctor said that Correll had a concussion and must be kept perfectly quiet for several days. Mr. and Mrs. Gomez said that he could stay with them till he recovered. Alex Gomez hated his enemy no longer. He and his wife did everything they could for his comfort. Bob Correll gradually recovered, but he did not recognize Gomez.

When the doctor said that Bob Correll could go back home, he said to Alex Gomez, "I must pay you folks for taking such good care of me."

"We don't want a cent," said Gomez. "I once stole a treasure from you that I must now return." He handed the Correll Bible back to Bob. Mr. Correll gazed at him and at the book, simply amazed.

Alex Gomez told Bob Correll all about the night that he had planned to ruin his life. He told him how he had taken the Bible instead, and how reading it and accepting Christ as Saviour had changed him completely. He ended his account by saying to Correll, "I never will forget your little girl's prayer that both you and I might listen to God and learn to love Him."

Bob Correll said, "Your story amazes me. Your life proves that what you say is true. I used to think the Bible was only for women and children. But since it has changed you so much, I am going to read it for myself. I realize that I need to be changed too."

THE LORD IS IN HIS HOLY TEMPLE

WM J. KIRKPATRICK

MOTHER DOESN'T LOVE US ANYMORE

"Trust in the Lord with all thine heart; and lean not unto thine own understanding." Proverbs 3:5

"Oh goody! Mother's coming home today!" shouted little Anna Finley, prancing about in her nightgown.

"Hurry up and get dressed," said Anna's big sister Hazel. We must have the house nice and everything ready to celebrate Mother's birthday."

Hazel was only fourteen but she had all the work to do as well as the care of her seven-year-old sister when their mother was away. Mrs. Finley had been a practical nurse before her marriage. When Mr. Finley died, the girls' mother went back to her nursing to support the family. Sometimes she had to be away several days at a time. When that happened Hazel and Anna missed her dreadfully.

Today was her birthday and she was coming home so both girls were delighted. They had planned the celebration for their mother's birthday for several days. They had made a big sign: "Welcome home! Happy Birthday!" and put it up on the wall. There was another "Welcome" sign too. It was on the mantel. The letters were made of jelly beans arranged carefully on a paper. The girls seldom got candy, but a kind neighbor had given Anna a small sack of jelly beans for her seventh birthday the week before. Instead of eating them, Anna had decided to save them for her mother's birthday. Anna had said to her big sister, "I love Mother so much I'm going to tell her to eat every one of my candies."

When Hazel looked at the jelly bean letters she had said to her little sister, "You can tell Mother that you want her to eat up her welcome, when you run to meet her. She will never guess what you mean till she comes in the house and sees your sign." Anna was delighted with the joke.

Now the two girls worked hard getting everything ready for the celebration. Hazel swept and mopped the floors; Anna dusted and put things away. Then she ran out to the garden to find the nicest flowers to decorate the table. While Hazel made the cake and got the meal ready Anna kept on bringing in more and more flowers. She put them in tumblers and jars and set them in every possible corner. Hazel did not interfere for she knew that their mother would appreciate all the love the flowers represented, even if they were not arranged in the most artistic manner.

Anna helped decorate the cake and set the table. Then when

all was ready the girls got out their carefully wrapped packages and placed them on their mother's plate.

"Won't Mother be surprised that you knitted her a scarf?" asked Anna. "She doesn't even know that you can knit, does she?"

"No," Hazel answered happily. "It was so nice of Mrs. Peters to show me how. I'm sure Mother will be pleased. And I know she will like the potholders you made, Anna. You did very neat work for a girl of your age."

Since all was now ready the girls went to the window to watch for their mother. By and by Anna said, "I wish Mother would hurry up and come. Why does it take her so long? I thought the sick lady was better now."

"She must be on the way home," said Hazel. "She might have just missed a bus. The busses don't run out here very often. If Mother only had a car she would be home in half the time."

Why doesn't Mother get a car then," asked Anna a little crossly.

"Mother doesn't have enough money to buy a car," said Hazel. "You know since Daddy went to heaven, Mother has to earn all the money."

"Why did God take Daddy to heaven?" was Anna's next question.

"I don't know," said Hazel.

"I don't think God was kind to take Daddy away," said Anna.

"Don't ever say that, Anna," said Hazel. "God is always kind. We don't know why He does some things, but He is always good. He sent His Son to die for our sins. You know Mother always says, 'We must trust in the Lord whether we understand what He does or not.' "

Suddenly Anna cried out, "There's Mother" and they both rushed out the door and over the field as fast as they could go to meet her. When Hazel realized that she was getting ahead of her little sister she stopped and grabbed her hand. Then the two of them were going so fast Anna's feet hardly seemed to touch the ground. All the girls could think of was the joy of having Mother with them again. They could hardly wait to have her clsap them in her arms.

At last beaming and breathless they had almost reached her. But just then their mother called out loudly, "Don't come near me! Don't touch me! Go back to the house!" Then she hurried towards the house herself keeping as far from her two girls as possible.

Hazel and Anna were too astonished to speak. They did not even move for a minute. Then they walked slowly back to the house hand in hand.

When they got back into the front room all decorated with flowers and looked at the table and the presents all ready for the celebration, Anna began screaming and crying. Hazel tried to put her arms around her little sister to comfort her but Anna pulled away and screamed out "Mother doesn't love us any more! Mother doesn't love us any more!"

"Oh, yes, she does. I'm sure Mother still loves us," said Hazel though she was almost crying herself. "Mother must be very tired or something. I don't know why she acted like that but there must be some reason. I'm sure she still loves us."

"But she said, 'Don't come near me! Don't touch me!'" sobbed Anna. "She used to hug us and say how glad she was to be home with us again."

"I know," said Hazel. "I don't understand it. But Mother has been so kind to us all our lives, I'm sure she wouldn't stop loving us. We must trust her Anna, and I think she will explain it to us by and by."

"I surely will, my poor darlings," said Mrs. Finley, coming into the room and putting her arms around them like she always did. "On my way home I stopped a moment to see our dear friend, Mrs. Peters. Her boy Robin had become very ill so I stayed with her till the doctor came. He said that Robin is coming down with a bad case of Scarlet Fever. When I came home I still had on the clothes I was wearing in their house. I had taken Robin's temperature and bathed his forehead, so I didn't dare let you girls get near me or touch me till I had bathed and changed all my things. I did not want to bring infection to you."

"Oh," said Anna, drawing a long breath. "Do you love us just as much as ever?"

"Of course, I do," said Mrs. Finley, hugging Anna again. "Surely you know, nothing could ever make me stop loving you."

"I know it now," said Anna, "but when you told us to go away, I thought you didn't love us any more. Hazel said you did, but I didn't believe her."

"Mrs. Finley looked very lovingly at her eldest daughter. "Perhaps it was easier for Hazel to trust me because she has known me longer," she said. "Or maybe it is because she has learned to trust the Lord."

"Maybe both," said Hazel smiling happily at her mother. Then she added, "How is Mrs. Peters feeling, Mother? It must be very hard for her because Robin is her only child."

"We must all pray that Robin will get better, if it is the Lord's will," said Mrs. Finley. But I will never forget what Mrs. Peters said. She said, 'I can trust my Saviour to do what is best for Robin and me."

"I have trusted the Lord to be my Saviour," said Hazel, "but I'm not sure I trust Him as much as Mrs. Peters does."

"Those who know the Lord best trust Him with all their hearts," said her mother. "I want us all to be in that number. But now tell me about all the beautiful decorations I see around the house."

After that they had a very happy celebration of their mother's birthday.

When they went to bed that night Anna said to Hazel, "I'm going to trust the Lord too. I'll never, never say again that God is not kind. And I'll never, never say again, "Mother doesn't love us anymore."

ISLAND PRISONER

Part 1

"No man can serve two masters." Matthew 6:24

"Oh, Jack, I hate Aunt Rachel! Do I really have to live with her and Uncle Otto while you are gone?" asked twelve-year-old Maidie.

"It seems the only thing to do," said her brother, Jack. "I have to go to England to see about the property Uncle Arthur left us. As soon as I can sell it, I will come back. The lawyer says it should bring more than enough to pay off the mortgage on our home. If we can't pay that, we will lose our place, Maidie, and you wouldn't like that."

"No, of course not," said Maidie. "But I want so much to go with you."

"I know you do," said Jack kindly. "And I would like so much to have you, but we don't have enough money."

"But you said you don't know how soon you will get back," said Maidie, half crying.

"That's true," said Jack. "I can't tell how long it will take to get everything settled. But you know I will come back as quickly as I can. It is very kind of Uncle Otto and Aunt Rachel to let you stay with them while I am gone. Be sure to obey them and do try to like Aunt Rachel. Don't forget that you promised to read a little from the Bible every day."

"I'll try to remember," said Maidie. "But, oh, I wish I could stay with anyone but Aunt Rachel."

The next day Jack took Maidie to their Uncle's house and he left for England.

Three years before, their parents had been killed in an accident. When this had happened their Uncle and Aunt had offered to let Maidie come and live with them. But Maidie begged Jack to let her stay with him. She did not like her aunt and she loved Jack with all her heart. Since Maidie and Jack lived in a college town, Jack told the relatives that they had decided to stay together. He explained that he would go to college when Maidie was in school, and would watch over her the rest of the time. Aunt Rachel and Uncle Otto said that this was a very poor arrangement. Jack was too young to have charge of his sister. But Jack and Maidie did not change their plans.

In order to get enough money for Jack to go through college the parents had mortgaged their home. Their accident had occurred less than a year later and ever since then Jack had been wondering how he could pay the mortgage when it became due. Now he had graduated and was looking for a position when the letter came from England.

Jack had accepted Christ as his Saviour while his parents were still living but Maidie had not. She went to Sunday School and church with Jack but when he talked with her about accepting Christ she said, "If I became a Christian I would have to do what God wants me to do. I want to do what *I* want to do.".

Maidie hated living with Aunt Rachel just as much as she had thought she would. She was an untidy girl and Aunt Rachel was extremely neat so she scolded Maidie constantly.

One afternoon just before dinner Maidie was sitting in the front room reading a story book when her aunt entered. Maidie had just come in from a run on the beach. "Where does your sweater belong?" Aunt Rachel asked crossly.

"Oh," said Maidie, "I forgot to put it away." She picked up her sweater which she had left lying on a chair and started up to her room.

"Wash your hands and brush your hair," called her aunt. "Don't come to dinner looking like a Shetland pony as you did yesterday."

Maidie felt cross as she brushed her hair. "Aunt Rachel is always finding fault with me," she said to herself. "I've only been here three days. How can I stand to live here all the time Jack is away?" Just then her eye fell on her Bible lying on the dresser, "Oh, dear! I promised Jack I'd read something every morning. I forgot today."

Maidie opened her Bible while she brushed her hair. On the page where it opened she saw these words, "No man can serve two masters."

"Oh," said Maidie, "I don't want to serve Satan, but I don't want to serve God either. I want to please myself."

"Hurry up, Maidie," called her aunt impatiently. So Maidie hurried down to dinner.

After dinner, Maidie went into the front room. "Where's that story book, Aunt Rachel?" she asked.

"I've put it away," said her aunt. "You never do anything all day long but read story books or amuse yourself in some other way."

"I want to finish reading that story," said Maidie. "Uncle Otto said I could read anything I like that was in the book case."

"Your uncle wasn't thinking of those books on the bottom shelf," said her aunt. "Those are Ann's books, but she didn't take them with her when she got married. I'm going to put them all away. Ann read story books once in a while, but she always helped me with the work. You never offer to help me with the dishes or anything. If you had lived with me for the last three years, you would be a very different girl from what you are now. It's Jack's fault that you are selfish, lazy, and untidy."

"It's not Jack's fault!" cried Maidie. "Jack is the nicest person in the world and you're the meanest."

"Go to your room," said Aunt Rachel sternly, "and stay there. I don't wish to see you before morning."

Maidie dashed to her room, but she did not stay there. As soon as she heard her aunt go into the kitchen she grabbed her coat and ran out of the house and down to the beach. Maidie was very, very angry with her aunt but she was angry with herself too. She thought her aunt was as hateful as she could be but she knew that she had not done anything to help. She remembered Jack's words, "It's kind of our relatives to let you stay with them."

Maidie ran along the beach, not caring where she was going. All she wanted was to get as far away from her aunt as possible. She ran much farther than she had ever been before. Suddenly she realized that she was all tired out. So she looked about her for a place to rest. She was in a cove beneath a high cliff much too steep to climb. Several fishing boats were anchored in the cove. One was pulled up on the beach so that it was partly out of the water. It was covered with a black tarpaulin which was pulled over some lumpy things. No one was around, so Maidie peeked under the tarpaulin. The boat was packed with barrels, but there was room between them for her to get in. Maidie got in, pulled the tarpaulin over her and lay down in the bottom of the boat to rest. There was no sound at all but the gentle lapping of the waves. Maidie lay there thinking. Her aunt would expect her to apologize the next morning. She knew she ought to but she did not want to. Her aunt had said horrid things about her and she had even said she blamed Jack.

Maidie woke up with a start. Two men were talking and waves were splashing against the sides of the boat. Maidie peeked out from the tarpaulin and saw that it was almost dark and the boat seemed to be out in the water. The tide had come further in while she slept and now these men were taking the boat out to sea. Maidie was too far from the shore to jump out of the boat, what should she do?

"Jarum," said one of the men, "We'll put the sail up now."

"What shall I do?" thought Maidie. "The men must have come to go fishing while I was asleep. They might be angry with me for getting into their boat. Maybe they won't see me. When they take the boat back to the shore, they'll go away again and then I can get out and run home." But how soon would they go back? Maidie was terrified but she kept perfectly still and listened.

The same man spoke again, "Jarum, hand me some more whiskey."

Then the other man spoke. He said, "Daniel, I kind of want to get out of this business. My mother would be much happier if I were just a plain fisherman."

The other man answered, "Nonsense, Jarum, she's old. You don't have to pay attention to her. You're young and you want to have a good time. You'll never get rich by fishing. There's good money in hauling liquor to the islands. We can sell it cheaper than the fishermen can get it anywhere else and still make a good profit."

"I know," said Jarum, "but the sheriff may catch us and then instead of getting rich, we'll land in jail. He's been snooping around the islands too much lately to suit me."

"Maybe we had better move the casks to some cave on the mainland," said Daniel. "Then if he finds our cave it will do no harm. Empty caves tell no tales."

The men continued talking and at last, in spite of her fears, Maidie fell asleep again.

Early the next morning she was wakened by a strange noise. For a moment she couldn't think where she was. Then she remembered that she was in a boat belonging to someone else. What was making the noise? Maidie soon found out what it was. The barrels in the boat were being rolled down a plank onto a dock below. One after another was taken away till there was a gap made and then a man's face looked at Maidie in astonishment.

Maidie was sitting up in the bottom of the boat. Her eyes were open wide with terror and her hair was tumbled around her in wild confusion.

"Daniel," called Jarum. "There's a real live mermaid in our boat."

"Oh, no, no," cried Maidie jumping up. "I'm not a mermaid. I only got into your boat to rest and I fell asleep till you were out in the water."

"Come out of there," called Daniel, and grabbing her arm roughly he made her jump from the boat to the dock.

"Don't be rough to the mermaid," said Jarum. "She's frightened and cold."

"You're a fool," said Daniel. Then he said to Maidie, "Who are you and where did you come from? Have you been in the boat all night?"

"Yes," said Maidie. "I didn't mean any harm. I only got into your boat to rest but I fell asleep. I wish I hadn't. My name is Madeline Darrel and just now I live with my uncle at Spruce Bay. My uncle is Mr. Otto Fisher."

"So that's who you are," said Daniel gruffly. "What did you hear us talking about while you were in our boat?"

"You were talking about taking whiskey to the islands," said Maidie.

"That's enough," said Daniel fiercely. He turned and talked with Jarum a couple of minutes. Then he said to Maidie, "You come with me."

"Oh no!" exclaimed Maidie, backing away. "Please take me back to Spruce Bay in your boat. I'm sure Uncle Otto will pay you if you bring me back."

"He'd likely pay me by putting me in jail," growled Daniel.

"Go along with him," said Jarum kindly. "He's not going to harm you. But he can't take you back to your uncle. Your uncle is the sheriff, you know, and he'd get us into trouble if he knew our business."

Just then a young teen-ager came running up. "I'm so glad you're back, Father," he said. "Grandmother is always worried till you get home again."

"Haco," said Jarum, "Here's a young lass your father is going to keep for a while. Speak to her. Maybe she'll go with you. She doesn't want to go with your father."

"Haco," said Daniel, "I can't come home till we get this cargo taken care of. Go home and tell Mother I'm back safe and take this girl with you."

So Haco turned to Maidie. "Will you come home with me to see Grandmother?" he asked.

Maidie looked at Haco's honest face and decided to go with him. She followed him up a cliff and along a little path till they came to a small house.

As soon as Haco opened the door a weak voice asked, "Is that you, Haco? Is your father back safe?"

"Yes, the boat's in," said the boy, "and Father's all right. He sent me home with a lass he found in the boat this morning."

"Bring her over here where I can see her," said the old lady. I haven't felt well enough to get up yet this morning."

Maidie stepped up to the bed at once and said, "I'm so glad you are here. I was afraid of those fishermen. May I stay with you till I can go home again?"

"Yes," said the old lady, "but tell me how you came to be in Daniel's boat."

"I got in to rest and then fell asleep," said Maidie. "When I woke up the boat was on the sea. Haco's father won't let me go home because I heard them talking about barrels of whiskey. My uncle is the sheriff and he thinks I would tell him about it, but I won't. You'll make him take me home, won't you?"

"I'll speak to Daniel about you, child," said the old lady, "but I can't promise."

"What is the name of this place?" asked Maidie.

"This is Deer Island," said Haco, as he brought in a tray containing tea and toast for his grandmother.

"Why I often looked at Deer Island from my bedroom window at Aunt Rachel's," exclaimed Maidie. "It can't be very far from Spruce Bay."

"We are less than twenty knots from Spruce Bay," said Haco, "but there is no boat service to our island. And Father's the only one on the island who takes his boat over there."

"You will persuade him to take me home, then, won't you?" said Maidie.

"If anyone can, it will be Grandmother," said Haco.

"You will, won't you?" said Maidie turning to the grandmother again.

"I will certainly do my best," said the old lady. "Now you and Haco had better eat breakfast."

They had just finished breakfast when Daniel came in. He went up to the bed and spoke more gently than Maidie had thought possible. "I'm back safe again, Mother." Then he sat down and ate his breakfast.

As soon as Daniel was through breakfast Grandmother called to him. She said, "You will take the girl home again, Daniel, won't you?"

"I can't do that, Mother," said Daniel. "I'd just be asking for trouble. I think the sheriff is suspicious of me already."

Grandmother said, "You know how much I want you to quit that business." As Daniel did not answer she went on, "But won't you get into trouble for keeping the girl here?"

"I'm not keeping her," said Daniel. "She got herself here and she can get herself back again. I'll not stop her, but I won't take her back myself, so don't ask me to."

When Maidie heard what Daniel had said she did not cry as Grandmother had feared. She said, "I must get back before my brother Jack returns from England. But I wasn't happy living with

Aunt Rachel. Since you and Haco are here I think it may be fun to be a prisoner on this island for a while."

ISLAND PRISONER

Part 2

"Seek ye out of the book of the Lord and read."

Maidie had to sleep in the store room of the little cottage. Haco carried nearly everything in it out to the woodshed. Then with driftwood he made her a rough sort of bed. Although this room was not nearly so nice as the one she had at Aunt Rachel's, Maidie liked it far better because Haco and his grandmother were so kind.

Maidie had found out at their very first breakfast that Haco was a Christian. He had bowed his head and returned thanks to God just as her brother Jack always did.

Haco milked the cows night and morning. He worked in the garden and did things in the house to help Grandmother, as Maidie soon learned to call the old lady. Haco seemed to be busy and happy all the time.

Grandmother worked too, but much more slowly, as she was very frail. Maidie soon loved Grandmother with all her heart. She was sweet and gentle and full of the love of Christ. Grandmother seemed better these days than she was when Maidie first arrived. Haco said Grandmother was always worse when his father was away on a trip.

When her work was done Grandmother would get her large print Bible on her knee and read it with great enjoyment. Sometimes she sat outdoors looking at the sea, but always with her big Bible. This did not seem strange to Maidie.

But it did seem strange to Maidie that Haco loved his Bible so much. Of course Jack loved his Bible, but he had always liked to read. There was nothing to read in Haco's small house but the Bible. Haco was fond of fishing, swimming and all sorts of outdoor activities. When his work was done he was always doing something active and he was pleased when Maidie joined him. But Haco never failed to get his Bible out after supper, and he read it for quite a while.

Life on the Island was pleasant except when Daniel was around. But he usually came home late and left early in the morning, and some nights he did not come home at all.

One bright sunny morning Haco said to Maidie, "Grandmother says she is feeling fairly well today. And the work is pretty well done. Would you like to go with me to see Dot Island? We can gather sea gull eggs there. I'm sure Jarum will let us use his boat."

"Oh, I'd love to," exclaimed Maidie.

Just then Daniel came down from the attic, where for once he had slept late. "You're not going anywhere today," he said to Haco. "I'm going to fence off some more pasture and you'll have to help me."

"All right, Father," said Haco pleasantly. Then he smiled at Maidie. "I'm sure we can go some other time."

Maidie said nothing, but she thought Daniel was hateful. And she couldn't understand how Haco could take their disappointment so cheerfully. She asked Haco about it that evening after Daniel had gone out.

Haco answered, "The Bible says, 'Children, obey your parents in all things, for this is well pleasing unto the Lord.' "

"But you're not a child," said Maidie.

"No," said Haco, "but I am my father's child and I want always to please the Lord because he has done so much for me."

"I don't see how the Lord has done so much for you," said Maidie. "Your mother died when you were a baby and your grandfather is dead too. Besides you don't have much money." She wanted to add, "And your father is not very nice," but she was afraid that Haco wouldn't like that.

"Why, Maidie," said Haco in surprise. "I have a happy home with my dear grandmother, and I have everything that I need. But I was thinking how the Lord Jesus died for my sins, so that I could go to heaven instead of to hell, where I deserve to go."

"I don't believe you deserved to go to hell," said Maidie. "I never knew anyone more good and unselfish than you are."

"Maidie," said Haco solemnly, "I was a great sinner. The Lord Jesus said, 'Thou shalt love the Lord thy God with all thy heart, and with all thy soul, and with all thy mind. This is the first and great commandment. And the second is like unto it, Thou shalt love thy neighbor as thyself.' I broke the two greatest commandments. Doesn't that make me a great sinner?"

"I suppose so," said Maidie slowly. She thought about Haco's words after she went to bed. She realized at last that she was a great sinner for she had never even wanted to obey either of those commandments.

The next morning dawned fair and blue and this time there was nothing to hinder the trip to Dot Island, if Jarum could lend them his boat that day.

When they reached the beach, there was Jarum sitting beside his nets, but instead of mending them he was playing with his cat. He jumped to his feet when he saw his visitors. "Maybe I think too much of that cat," he said.

His mother had just come out. "Indeed you do," she said. Then she turned to Maidie, "Jarum risked his life to save that cat. Wasn't that a foolish thing to do?"

Jarum said, "Well, I saw that poor cat clinging to the mast of a sunken ship out in the bay. The life guards had rescued the crew before the ship went down but I guess no one thought of the poor cat. There was a pretty bad storm, but I couldn't bear to see the cat drowned, so I went out in my boat and rescued it."

"Think of that," said Jarum's mother. "My boy nearly lost his life saving a cat!"

"I think you are very brave," said Haco looking admiringly at Jarum. "Weren't you afraid to go out alone in your boat in a storm?"

"I didn't think about that," said Jarum. "I was just thinking about the poor cat. I guess I should have thought about it though. I don't want to leave my mother all alone, and besides I am not ready to die."

"I wouldn't like to go out in a boat in a bad storm," said Haco. "But I don't need to be afraid to die. I know my Saviour would take me to heaven. Before I die though, I want to do something for Jesus."

"You do good things all the time, Haco," exclaimed Maidie. "I don't know what Grandmother would do without you."

"Those are just little things," said Haco. "I would like to do something big for Jesus before I die." "But," he added, "if Jarum is willing to lend us his boat today, we better go after those gull eggs right away. Grandmother asked us to be home before sundown.

Jarum was agreeable and they set out in his boat. Maidie was pleased that Haco let her try to row. It took her a little while to get into the swing of it, but soon they were going along smoothly.

In less than an hour they reached the rocky little island where thousands of gulls nested. They pulled their boat up on the beach, and started climbing up the rocks. The sea gulls flew up into the air with wild cries as Haco and Maidie filled their basket with eggs.

34

They were careful to take only one or two eggs from each nest so that no gull would be unhappy after they left. Haco told Maidie that each egg would be tested before it was used in cooking. The eggs would be set in a pan of well water. The good eggs would lie on the bottom and the bad eggs would float.

After they had filled their baskets, Maidie and Haco sat on one of the rocky ledges and looked out at the beautiful scenery. Suddenly Maidie exclaimed, "Haco, did you see what that gull did! It got a clam down on the beach and then flew high up in the air with it. Then it dropped the clam down on the beach and swooped down after it. Was it playing?"

"No," said Haco. "Sea gulls often do that. When the clam falls on the rocks below it breaks the shell so the gull can eat the meat."

"How can they ever find their clams again down there among all those rocks?" asked Maidie.

"God has given them wonderful eyes," said Haco. "If they could not break clam shells in some way, many of them would starve to death."

Before they started back, Maidie said to Haco, "Why do you like to read the Bible so much?"

"I like to read it because God is speaking to me. He tells me things He wants me to know, and things He wants me to do, and things He wants me not to do. I like best of all to read about Jesus my Saviour. We never can half pay Him back for loving us and for dying for us. But at least we can try to please Him every day."

"That's why you are always helping," said Maidie thoughtfully.

"I've never done much for Jesus," said Haco, "but perhaps He'll give give me something big to do for Him some day."

When they reached home Grandmother smiled a welcome and exclaimed over their baskets of eggs.

Haco went out to get some wood. In a moment he was back again. "Come out, Maidie," he called, "And look at the sunset. It's just beautiful." Maidie followed him out and he pointed at the golden sky reflected in the water below. "That looks like the pathway to heaven, doesn't it?"

"It's the most beautiful sunset I ever saw," said Maidie, "but why does it make you think about heaven?"

"My mother is there and my grandfather is there," said Haco. Grandmother and I are going to be there. And we pray every day that Father and Jarum will come to Jesus so that they will go there too. And," Haco added reverently, "my Master is there. Seeing Him will be best of all."

"When you speak of your Master, you mean Jesus, don't you," said Maidie.

"Yes," said Haco. "Is Jesus *your* Master, Maidie?"

"No," said Maidie. "I didn't want to belong to Jesus because I wanted to have a good time first. But you and Grandmother and my brother Jack are much nicer and much happier than the people who do not belong to Him. So now I wish He *was* my Master."

"You can ask Him to be your Master right now, Maidie," said Haco earnestly.

Maidie stood quite still for a minute. Then she said, "I will." She went into her little room and knelt down by her driftwood bed. She prayed, "Oh God, I am a great sinner, but Jack always says You are a great Saviour. Thank You for dying for my sins. Please come into my heart and make me Your child. Please help Jack to find me when he comes home. And please be my Master always. For Jesus' sake, Amen."

When Maidie got up from her knees, she knew that God had heard her prayer. Now the Lord Jesus was her Saviour and her Master. How happy this would make Jack when he heard about it!

Maidie woke up early the next morning. She heard Haco go out to milk the cows. She thought, "Haco is always doing something to please the Lord. And I lie lazily in bed till breakfast time. But now the Lord Jesus is my Master too." She jumped out of bed and dressed quickly. Then she knelt down and prayed. After that she went out to help Grandmother.

Maidie helped Grandmother that day till all the work was done. When they had finished she went and sat by the old lady. She said to her "I'm very glad I came to Deer Island. Now the Lord Jesus is *my* Master. And it's all because of you and Haco."

"I'm so glad you belong to Jesus now," said Grandmother putting her arm around Maidie. Then she added, "Be sure to read a little in the Bible every day. That is the way to learn to know your new Master, and to find out what He wants you to do."

"Jack asked me to read a little in the Bible every day. I tried to remember to do it to please Jack. But now I *want* to read it, only I can't, because my Bible is still at Aunt Rachel's."

"Read mine whenever you like," said Grandmother quickly.

Maidie hugged the old lady and after that she borrowed Grandmother's Bible every day and sometimes even more often.

As time went by Maidie did more and more of the work as Grandmother was getting feeble. Often Grandmother said, "I am sure the Lord sent you here. I don't know what we would do without you."

Maidie always answered, "If Jack were only here, I would be

perfectly happy." As the days went by she became more and more concerned, thinking that Jack might have come back and that he would not know where to find her. But she tried to turn her worries into prayers to the God she was beginning to know.

One day Daniel told his mother that he was going on another trip the next morning and would be away two or three days. He said, "If a storm should come up I might have to stay on another island till it was over, so don't worry about me if I am gone even longer."

His mother said, "I always worry when you are on that sort of trip. The Bible says, 'Woe unto him that giveth his neighbor drink.' How can I help worrying when God has pronounced woe upon you?"

"You're the best little mother in the world," said Daniel, "but don't preach at me." Then he went out.

"Haco," said Grandmother, "I'm sure that Daniel expects Jarum to go with him. Jarum's mother says that he doesn't want to go but he hates to say "No," to your father. It breaks my heart that Daniel is leading Jarum wrong. Maybe you could persuade Jarum not to go."

"I'll try," said Haco. "Will you come with me, Maidie?"

Soon they were at the little house down by the beach. Maidie stroked Jarum's cat and listened.

Haco said, "Don't go with Father tomorrow morning, Jarum. The Bible says, 'Woe unto him that giveth his neighbor drink.' Your mother is always sad when you go on that sort of trip. And my grandmother is sad too. She hates to have Father go and she feels very sad that Father is leading you wrong."

"I know I shouldn't go," said Jarum. "Mother is always telling me how God hates the liquor business. But I don't like to offend your father. If he stopped visiting me, I would be very lonely."

"If you would come to Jesus, He would always be with you," said Haco. The Bible tells us that Jesus said, 'I will never leave thee, nor forsake thee.' "

"How did you ever learn so many Bible Verses?" asked Jarum.

"Sometimes I fasten a copy of a Bible verse to the plow and practice as I walk along behind. Other times I put one above the sink where I wash out the milk cans."

"You must love the Bible a lot to go to all that trouble," said Jarum.

"I do," said Haco. "And you would too if you would accept Christ as your Saviour. Won't you, Jarum?"

"I'll think about it," Jarum answered.

"You won't go with Father tomorrow?" Haco asked anxiously."

After a moment's hesitation, Jarum said, "I'll say 'No' to your father this time. I know my mother will be glad when I tell her I'm not going."

When the young folks told Grandmother that Jarum had promised not to go with Daniel the next day, Grandmother said, "Thank God."

ISLAND PRISONER

Part 3

**"Thy word have I hid in my heart that I might
not sin against Thee." Psalm 119:11**

Daniel did not go on his trip after liquor the next day as Jarum refused to go with him. But he did not give up the idea. He went to another island and persuaded a young fellow there to go with him the following week.

Grandmother was disappointed. She had hoped that if Jarum refused to go, Daniel would give up the idea. She lost her appetite and spent most of her time praying for him and reading her Bible. Maidie was well able to do all the work and she did it cheerfully.

The morning after Daniel left Grandmother was unable to rise from her bed. After the work was done Maidie came and sat by her side to read the Bible.

"Would you read it aloud, Dear?" asked Grandmother. "My eyes are too dim to read today."

"I would love to," said Maidie. "Where would you like me to read?"

"I would like to hear Psalm sixteen," said the old lady. Maidie read it. Grandmother thanked her and said, "Please read the next one too." Maidie read Psalm seventeen also. Grandmother closed her eyes as she listened. When Maidie had finished she opened her eyes and with a radiant face repeated the last verse from memory, "As for me, I will behold Thy face in righteousness. I shall be satisfied when I awake with Thy likeness." Then she said, "Thank you, Maidie. I think I will sleep a little now."

"Grandmother is asleep," said Maidie as she joined Haco outside.

"Do you think she is ill?" asked Haco anxiously.

"No, I don't think so," said Maidie. "She is always frightened when your father is away on one of his trips. I think she will be all right when he gets back."

"There's going to be a storm," said Haco, looking anxiously at the sky, where black clouds were rapidly moving together.

"I would like to see the sea in a storm," said Maidie. "Couldn't we go down to Jarum's place and see the big waves?"

"Not tonight," said Haco. "I don't think it will begin here till early morning."

"Let's go to bed now," said Maidie. "Then we can go down to Jarum's place as soon as it is light. We could come home in time to milk and get breakfast."

Early the next morning Haco knocked on Maidie's door. She jumped up and opened it a crack. "Grandmother is still sleeping," he said. "If you want to go to Jarum's we better start now. The wind is pretty strong but I think we can make it. The storm is worse on the sea than on the land."

In five minutes Maidie was ready. Haco handed her his waterproof coat and cap to put on. "You wear these," he said. "I'll wear Father's old ones."

When they stepped out into the wind it was barely light enough to see. They held hands so that they would not be blown away. "It's a good thing the wind is coming from the sea," said Maidie. "Otherwise we might be blown over the cliff."

It gradually grew lighter. Suddenly Haco said, "There's a boat on the rocks. I can't see it very well. I hope it isn't Father's." Maidie looked at the rocks but she could only see something dark against them.

Just before they reached Jarum's house Haco said, "It's not Father's boat. I don't know whose boat it is, but I wish we could do something to save the men. Their boat won't last an hour in this storm. If Jarum goes, I'll go with him."

Jarum came rushing out of his house just as they got there. "We must try to save them," he shouted as he started pushing his boat down into the water. Instantly Haco started pushing also. Then Jarum jumped in and grabbed an oar. Haco jumped in behind him and grabbed the other oar. Maidie jumped in unnoticed for both Jarum and Haco were battling to get the boat started toward the wreck. Both the wind and the waves were against them. When they got the boat headed in the right direction, they began rowing with all their might.

"Are you frightened, Haco?" called Jarum. He had to shout because the wind and the waves made so much noise.

"No," Haco called back. "But I wish Maidie had stayed on shore."

Jarum stopped rowing for a minute. "Maidie," he shouted, "what are you doing here? I wouldn't have brought you along for anything."

Maidie did not try to answer. She knew she could not make herself heard if she tried. She did not realize the danger of being out in such a storm in a row boat. She felt safe with both Haco and Jarum on board.

Jarum called to Haco, "There's no time to take her back. We have the tide with us now. We should be there in five minutes." He started rowing again.

When they got near the doomed boat they saw two men clinging to its side. For a moment Jarum wondered what to do. He dared not row close to the wreck for fear his boat would be driven on the rocks also.

A slight lull in the storm allowed him to row closer. "Jump," shouted Jarum, and one of the men leaped into the boat and sank down in the bottom exhausted. Jarum's boat moved away with the shock. He and Haco were trying to row back again to get the other man when another piece of the wrecked boat went down.

"We dare not go nearer," said Jarum. "The only chance of saving that man is to swim to him with one end of the rope." He was unwinding the rope on his boat as he spoke. "If I don't make it back, Haco," he said, "be good to my mother."

"Maidie," said Haco speaking into her ear, "I'm going instead of Jarum. I'm ready, he isn't. Take care of Grandmother."

Just as Jarum finished unwinding the rope, Haco seized it, dropped off his coat and jumped overboard. "Haco, Haco, come back!" cried Maidie. But Haco battled on through the storm. He got close enough to the rocks for the half drowned man to grab the rope. Then the last part of the wreck went down. The man managed to cling to the rope while Jarum pulled it in. Jarum hauled him over the side of the boat and he sank unconscious to the bottom. But Haco did not make it back. As the last part of the wreck went down, Haco was pulled down with it and he did not come up again. That stormy day Haco went Home to be with the Master he loved and served.

When Jarum realized that it was impossible to rescue Haco, he sat immovable in his boat gazing at the rocks where Haco had gone down. Maidie sat in her place as if she had been turned to stone.

If the worst of the storm had not been over their boat would certainly have been swamped.

The first man that had been rescued, sat up and looked at Jarum. "I think I can help you row," he said. Then he struggled up beside Jarum and tood an oar. Mechanically Jarum pulled on the other oar. And the two of them finally got the boat back to shore.

Jarum's mother was standing on the shore crying. As soon as the boat stopped she said, "Jarum, I'm going to lock the door and hide the key to keep you in. I thought I would never see you again."

"Mother," said Jarum, "please make some hot coffee for the men we saved from the wreck." Then he and the man who had helped row, carried the still unconscious man into the house and laid him on Jarum's bed. As soon as the man had revived enough to swallow a spoonful of coffee, Jarum went in search of Maidie. She was still sitting unmoveable in the boat.

"Maidie," said Jarum, "you mustn't sit here in the cold and wet. You'll be sick. Let me help you out." But Maidie did not move.

Jarum got into the boat beside her. He said, "Haco is safe with God. Storms will never hurt him again. Then Jarum buried his face in his hands and sobbed. Maidie leaned her head on his shoulder but she did not speak. Soon Jarum looked at her. He saw that she had fainted. So he picked her up and carried her into the house. Maidie was put to bed there and Jarum's mother did everything she could for her. But Maidie ran a high fever for many days. She did not know where she was or who was taking care of her. But she sometimes called out "Haco, come back!" Other times she called "Jack, Jack, where are you?"

Ten days later Maidie wakened from a sleep which had lasted several hours. She looked at Jarum's mother. "Am I in your house?" she asked.

"Yes," said Jarum's mother. "You've been very sick, but please God, you'll get better now."

"Is it true?" asked Maidie. "Is Haco — " "Has he never come back?"

"He'll never come back to us, Maidie, but some day we will see him again in heaven," said Jarum's mother. Then she added, "Haco was the finest boy I ever knew."

But Maidie did not hear her. She had buried her head in the bed clothes and was sobbing wildly.

Jarum's mother went to the kitchen and said "She's herself now, but she's crying bitterly. Maybe you had better go to her, Jack."

His sister was still crying violently when Jack went into the room. He said, "Maidie, Maidie, don't you know who I am?"

Maidie stopped crying and gazed at him. He stooped to kiss her and she recognized him. She threw her arms around his neck and said, "Oh, Jack, stay with me. Don't go away. I'm so miserable."

"I won't go away till you are able to go with me," he said soothingly.

"How did you get here?" Maidie asked after a while.

"I was on the boat that got wrecked," said Jack. "And you were in the boat that saved me from drowning. But I did not know that. I have been very sick, too. It is only lately I learned that the sick girl Jarum's mother was taking care of was my lost little sister. I am so thankful to have found you again."

Later Jack said to her, "Now the mortgage is paid off and there is enough money left so that we can do something for these kind friends who have been taking care of us. I think you will soon be strong enough to go home with me to our own house."

"But, Jack, I can't leave Grandmother," said Maidie. "Who has taken care of her while I have been sick?"

"God has taken care of her," said Jack. "You know how hard it would have been for her to live without Haco. God spared her that. He called her to heaven before Haco got there. When Haco got to heaven he found his grandmother there to welcome him. Jarum went to their home to tell her the sad news. He found her lying in bed with a happy smile on her face and her open Bible beside her. But her spirit had gone to be with the Lord."

"It was better," said Maidie. "But I am so sorry I won't see her again." And she started to cry once more.

"Yes, you will," said Jack tenderly. "We will live near Haco and his grandmother forever and ever. I wish I could have known Haco. He saved my life at the cost of his own. But, Maidie, it makes me so happy to know that you and I will both be in heaven with them and with our dear parents. Jarum told me that you belong to the Lord Jesus now."

Just then Jarum knocked on the door. "May I come in?" he asked. "I haven't seen Maidie for a long time. But Mother says I mustn't stay more than a minute."

Maidie looked at him and said, "Where is the other man who was on that boat?"

"Daniel took him home to his family," said Jarum.

"Daniel did?" asked Maidie wonderingly. She had never known Daniel to do anything for someone else.

"Yes, Maidie," said Jarum. "Things are different here. Haco's

Master is now *my* Master and Daniel can say that, too." Jarum had tears in his eyes as he spoke but Maidie thought she had never seen him look so happy.

A few days after this Maidie and Jack went home. They visited Aunt Rachel and Uncle Otto and Maidie told them how sorry she was for the way she had acted when in their home.

The relatives were very happy to see Maidie for they had believed her drowned.

Things were different with Maidie now. She loved to go to Sunday School and church. She loved to read her Bible and memorize verses as Haco had done. She prayed every day that she might do things pleasing to her Master. Jack said that she had grown into a splendid housekeeper.

Jack and Maidie sometimes visited their island friends. Often, now, Daniel and Jarum went around the islands together. These times they did not take whiskey. They took God's message of salvation.

One day Maidie said to Jack, "I wonder if Haco knows that his death brought you back to me and it also brought both his father and Jarum to Christ."

"I do not know," said Jack, "But if he doesn't know yet, he surely will some day."

"I'll never forget Haco," said Maidie. "I want to please the Lord every day as long as I live, like he did. I'll never forget the look on Jarum's face when he said, 'Haco's Master is now *my* Master.' I want to help other people come to know the Saviour. I'm so glad the Lord Jesus became my Master, while I was a prisoner on Deer Island."

Adapted from "In an Isle of the Sea" now out of print.

THE BROKEN WINDOW

"Be ye doers of the word, and not hearers only,
deceiving your own selves." James 1:22

Jeff and his cousin Jim were in the same Sunday School class. Both boys were fifteen and each of them worked in a store after school and on Saturdays. Jeff worked in his father's dry goods store and Jim delivered groceries. Both boys were Christians and so they paid good attention in Sunday School. On this particular Sunday the lesson was about Ananias and Sapphira. Mr. Brian, their teacher said, "See how God hates lying. God is a God of truth. Over and over in the Bible we read that God loves truth and hates lying. And remember that an acted lie is as bad as a spoken lie. Ask God to give you a love for the truth and to keep you from ever spreading or acting a lie."

On the way home from church Jim said, "Wasn't that a good lesson we had in Sunday School? I get so much from Mr. Brian's class."

"It was a good lesson all right," said Jeff "but it would be very hard to practice. My Dad has such a fearful temper I almost have to lie at times to get on with him. When Mother was living she would take my part, but now I have no one to help. And I'm in an awful fix right now," he added gloomily. "Saturday night I accidentally broke a window while I was changing a display."

"Not one of the large front windows, I hope!" exclaimed Jim.

"Yes, one of the large front windows," answered Jeff. Father had already gone home so he doesn't know anything about it yet. He will be furious when he finds it is broken. I hope he will think some passer-by did it. I sure hope he doesn't ask me if I broke it. I don't want to lie but I would never dare to say Yes. If I said Yes, he would beat me black and blue."

Jim looked kindly at his cousin. "I know Uncle has a quick temper," he said, "but I am sure it is always best to tell the truth. If you ask God to help you tell the truth, He will help you. Remember our memory verse "The Lord is in His holy Temple, let all the earth keep silence before Him." God is greater than all the people in the world put together. He can make you brave and He can help your Dad not to be so angry."

Jim added, "I can guess how much you miss your mother. Since my mother went to heaven when I was three I don't miss her so much. But how I miss my Dad! He was such a wonderful Christian man."

"I wish my father was a Christian," said Jeff, "but he is a good father when he isn't angry."

The boys separated. Jim went back to the foster home where he had lived since his father died a few months earlier. Jeff went to the home he now shared alone with his father.

When Jeff reached the store the next afternoon, he found his father very angry. "Look at this, Jeff," his father exclaimed. "Some wretched idle fellow has broken one of our expensive front windows. I mean to find out who did it and he shall pay for it. If he hasn't any money he should be put in jail. Have you any idea who could have done such a thing?"

"No," said Jeff hastily. Then he wished with all his heart that he had not said it, but he dared not tell the truth.

"Well I'm going to find out who did it and then he had better look out," said Mr. Gray angrily.

"It might have been an accident," said Jeff miserably.

"How could anyone break a thick window like that by accident?" said his father. "Look there, you can see something has been banged into it. How could anyone walking along the sidewalk hit the window hard enough to break it by accident? I'll find out who did it and he'll be sorry ever after."

Jeff shivered and wondered for the hundredth time how he could have been so careless as to kick the window with his foot when he stood back to get the effect of the display he had just put in the window.

"Well there's no use you standing there looking at it," said his father. Mrs. Brian called up and asked if we could deliver the coat our alterations lady fixed for her. I said I would have you take it to her after school."

Jeff was thankful to get out of the store. He was glad to have an errand to the home of his Sunday School teacher for he had spent many a pleasant evening there. When he reached the house Mr. Brian came to the door and took the package. "Thank you," he said. Then he said, "Jeff, I would like you to know what an inspiration you and Jim are to me. You always seem so interested in the lesson. Having two fellows like you in the class helps the other boys to listen too. I appreciate it very much. You are a fine listener. I am sure you obey the words found in James 1:22, "Be ye doers of the word and not hearers only." I know you have to hurry back to the store now, but come to see us whenever you can. We know how much you miss your dear mother, and Mrs. Brian and I would like to feel that our place is a second home for you."

As Jeff walked back to the store his face was red. How kind

the Brians are, he thought. But if they knew that I had lied this very day they would not invite me to their home. I am not a doer of the word. Just yesterday we had a lesson on speaking the truth. I heard it but I have not done it.

As Jeff approached his father's store his cousin Jim was going in with some groceries. He left the door open as his hands were full. Mr. Gray did not hasten to close it as it was a warm afternoon. Jeff knew that his father had told the grocer that Jim might just as well leave their groceries at the store. This would save him a trip out to their place.

Jeff heard his father's voice still angry. "Look here, Jim. See what some rascal did to one of my expensive front windows? Would you have any idea who could have done it?"

"I did not break it," said Jim quickly. And he started out the door. But Mr. Gray thought there was something suspicious about Jim's manner.

"Wait a minute," he said roughly. "I didn't ask you if you broke it. I asked you if you had any idea who might have done it. Answer me."

Mr. Gray seized Jim by the shoulder. Jim did not answer. Mr. Gray shook him. "Look here," he said. "I think you do know something about it and you've got to tell me."

Jim was still silent. Jeff stood out of sight listening and trembling.

Jim was still silent. Mr. Gray shook him even more roughly. "You answer me. You're my nephew. I have a right to punish you when you are stubborn. I'll make you tell me what you know. I'll beat you. I'll call the police. I'll . . . "

Jeff rushed into the store. "Father, let Jim go. I broke the window and he doesn't want to tell on me."

Mr. Gray let go of him. He turned to his son. "You liar, you! You said you didn't have any idea who broke it. Wait till I get my hands on you."

A customer had just come into the store. Mr. Gray turned to wait on her while Jim stood beside Jeff. He did not have to leave just then because he had made his last delivery for the day. He hated to leave his cousin in such trouble.

The customer spoke in a low tone to Mr. Gray. She said, "I could not help hearing the conversation as I came in. I beg of you not to punish your son for what was plainly an accident."

Mr. Gray answered, "At least I'll punish him for lying to me."

"The lady said, "But he told you the truth himself just before I came in. Of course he should have told you the truth in the first place. But if you forgive him this time I believe he will always tell you the truth after this. You know, Mr. Gray, both your son and your nephew are known around this town as fine Christian boys. If Jeff had a Christian father to encourage him I think he would never lie again."

Then the lady bought what she wanted and left the store.

Mr. Gray walked over to where the two boys were standing. Jim said, "Uncle, won't you please forgive Jeff? He wouldn't have broken that window for anything."

"I'm afraid I treated you rather badly," said Mr. Gray to his nephew. "So since you ask it I'll forgive Jeff for your sake. I realize my temper sometimes gets the best of me. I believe I'll start going to church with Jeff. Maybe I'll find something there that will help me to control it."

Mr. Gray went over to check the cash register. Jeff said to Jim, "Thank you for sticking up for me. I'll never forget it and I will ask God every day to make me a doer of the word, as well as a hearer of it."

THAT OLD RED SWEATER

**"Be ye doers of the word, and not hearers only,
deceiving your own selves." James 1:22**

Dorene looked once more at her new pink formal with delight. It was the first time she had ever bought the most becoming dress she could find. Before that she had always bought the cheapest thing that would do, because money was scarce in their home. But now that Dorene was a senior in high school, her mother had agreed that she should have something really nice. Dorene had saved as much of her strawberry money from summer as she could, and added to it with what she earned baby-sitting. Then she and her mother had gone from store to store till they had found this pink formal which was a perfect fit and made Dorene look like a rose bud.

Dorene anticipated the admiration she would receive from her classmates. She was a popular girl, in spite of her Christian testimony, because she was good-tempered and friendly and always ready to help someone. Then there was Miss Drayton, her Domestic Science teacher. Dorene looked forward to her smile of approval. Miss Drayton seemed to take a special interest in her, praising her taste on several occasions. She knew Miss Drayton guessed that she often had to wear clothes which were bought only for their low price.

As Dorene put on her new dress for the Junior-Senior banquet, she felt thrilled. Her coat was shabby but she would stow that away in her locker, before going to the gym, where the tables were set up. When Dorene went downstairs, her mother said, "It's just perfect, isn't it?" Them a worried look came over her face. "It's such a chilly evening, you must have a wrap to wear during the banquet, if the gym should be cold."

"Oh I don't need anything," said Dorene. "Anyway I don't have anything decent."

"You better take something along," said Mrs. Forester. "Your appearance one evening isn't worth the risk of taking a bad cold."

"But, Mother, I haven't anything that would do at all," cried Dorene. "My slip-ons would look terrible, and muss my hair besides. My only cardigan is that old red sweater, which would look awful with this pink dress."

"If you wore it open, I don't think it would be very noticeable while you're sitting at the table. "I surely wish we could have gotten you a nice wrap. Since we couldn't, I want you to take your red

48

sweater. Take it with you to the gym. I hope you won't need to wear it, but I want you to keep it close enough to you so that you can slip it on, sooner than get a chill."

When Dorene reached the high school, she rushed her old coat into her locker. She was greatly tempted to put her sweater in with it, but she knew that would not be honoring her mother. As she hesitated a moment, Miss Drayton passed by. She stopped when she saw Dorene and exclaimed over her pretty dress. Then seeing the girl look ruefully at the sweater in her hand, she added, "That doesn't go very well with your dress, I know. But you better keep it with you as the gym is pretty cold tonight."

"Mother wanted me to keep it with me," said Dorene. Then she resignedly thrust her sweater under her arm and went to the gym where she deposited it on the nearest vacant chair. After that she hastened to join the gay group of boys and girls chatting together in the center of the great gym now decorated beautifully in blue and gold, the high school colors.

"Dorene, I didn't know you were so beautiful," exclaimed one of the girls. All eyes were turned on her with evident admiration. Dorene felt very happy and silently thanked the Lord for directing her to a dress so becoming and yet so modest that it would not in any way dim her testimony for Him.

When everyone sat down to the tables, Dorene retrieved her sweater, and hung it on a rung under her chair.

The food was delicious, the decorations beautiful, and Dorene sitting between two of her best friends was having a perfect time. However the gym was not warm, and the temperature seemed to be dropping. Girls began to slip on fancy wraps. Dorene wished she had anything fit to be seen, but she couldn't stand the thought of putting on that old red sweater. She drank a second cup of hot coffee, but even that did not warm her much. When she started eating the ice cream, cold chills ran up and down her spine. Then she thought of what her mother had said, "I want you to put on your sweater, rather than have you catch a bad cold."

"I'd rather catch a cold than put on that sweater," Dorene said to herself. "It will ruin the evening for me. Yet if I don't put it on it will displease the Lord." Dorene belonged to the Lord and she realized that she had no right to catch a cold for vanity's sake. Reluctantly she reached down, pulled up her sweater and put it on. No one appeared to notice so she felt a little better about it. The warmth began to feel comfortable, but still she couldn't quite banish from her mind the discontent with which she wore it. Why couldn't she have had a beautiful wrap to go with her dress? Many of the girls had several.

When everyone rose from the table, Dorene was tempted once more to take off her sweater, but she was still none too warm. In just a few minutes, she and the other Christian young people would be going home, as a dance was to follow. So Dorene bravely kept her sweater on till it was time to go.

As she was standing by her locker putting on her coat, Miss Drayton came past again. This time a tall well-dressed woman was with her. She stopped and introduced her pupil saying, "Miss Porter, this is Dorene Forester, one of my best students."

Miss Porter looked keenly at the girl. Then she said, "I would like to have an interview with you, Miss Forester, as to what you are going to do after you graduate. Have you time to talk with me now in Miss Drayton's office?"

"I'll drive you home afterwards," said Miss Drayton quickly.

"I guess so," said Dorene in surprise. Then she followed the two women upstairs, leaving the other students gazing after her in wonder.

Miss Porter came to the point immediately. "I am the head of The Women's Wear Designing company located on College Avenue. I am interested in taking girls with an aptitude for the work, as soon as they graduate from high school, and training them into my business. The pay is not large at first, but it increases steadily as they become more useful to the firm. Would you be interested in such a proposition?"

"Oh, I think it would be wonderful!" exclaimed Dorene. "Are you really offering me a position?"

"Yes, if you want it," answered Miss Porter. "I think you would suit me. Your teacher gives a good account of you. But what really attracted my attention to you was your red sweater."

"My red sweater," gasped Dorene.

"Yes," answered Miss Porter with a chuckle. "I had just remarked to Miss Drayton that people either had good taste, or hadn't, and there was nothing we could do about it. Then I spotted you. I said to her, 'See that girl. She is wearing a beautiful dress but the effect is spoiled by adding a sweater which just kills it.' Miss Drayton replied, 'No one knows that better than she, but she has the good sense to wear what she has, rather than catch cold.' I decided than and there that you were the girl to whom I would make my offer."

"Thank you so much," said Dorene. "Your work is what I would like best to do. But I never dreamed I could get into it as soon as I finish high school."

Before Dorene went to bed she thanked God that He had helped her to do what she knew was right, and for Miss Porter's offer.

She felt ashamed that she had worn her sweater so reluctantly when God was going to use it to arrange a wonderful future for her. She said to herself, "That old red sweater should remind me constantly to do God's will joyfully."

JESUS CHRIST IS COMING FOR ME

Tune: Fishers of Men

HARRY D. CLARKE
Har. by Talmage J. Bittikofer

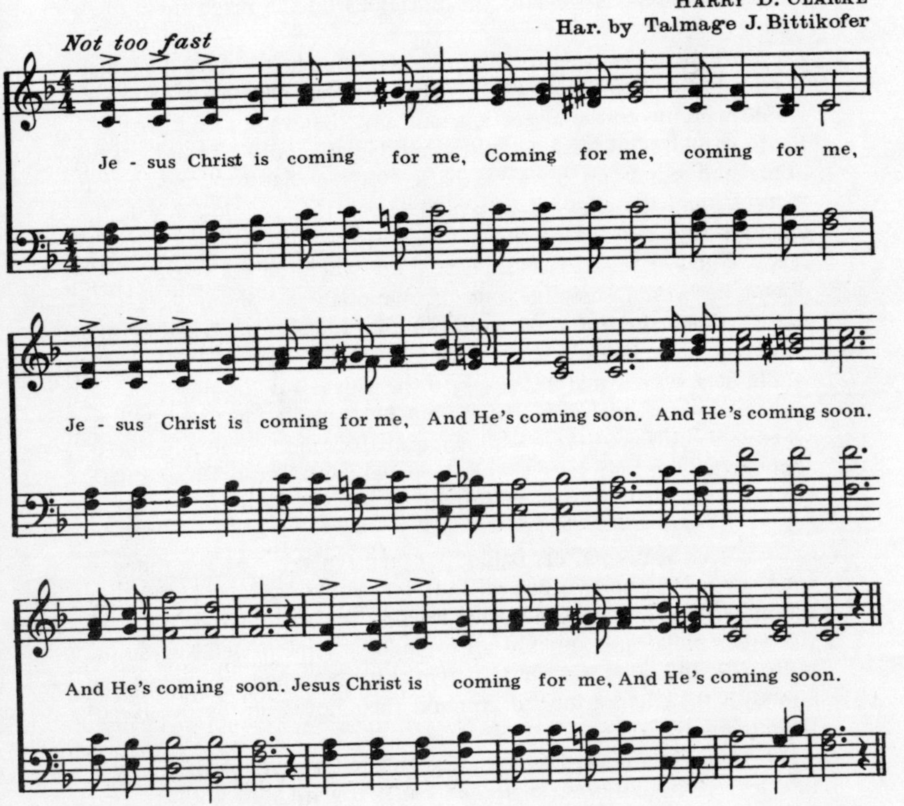

GULAB AND THE TIGER HUNT

"Behold I come quickly; and My reward is with Me, to give every man according as his work shall be." Revelation 22:12

Gulab's job was to take care of the thirty bull buffaloes that belonged to his village in India whenever there was no work for them to do for the villagers. Gulab was only a small boy but he did his job well. Every morning he took the buffaloes to graze in the fields outside the village and to wallow in the huge mudhole they found there. And every evening Gulab brought these huge animals back into the village. Gulab was kind to the buffaloes but he made them obey him.

When it was time for them to start out in the morning Gulab would shout "Stand in rows." Then when they were all lined up, he would walk up to the biggest one and say "Bend your neck, Baldo." Baldo would bend his head down, and Gulab would grab hold of his horns and climb up onto his back. After that he would shout "March" and the whole herd would march to the fields outside the village where they spent the day eating grass or wallowing in the mud. Gulab would play beside them but when the sun started to go down, he would scramble out of the mud and shout "Stand in rows." Then the buffaloes would line up once more, Gulab would climb up onto Baldo's back and again shout "March." Then the whole herd would march back into the village for the night.

One day Gulab was playing on the bank beside the mud hole where the buffaloes were wallowing in the mud. Suddenly one of them stood up and gave a low deep bellow. Two or three others stood up and bellowed also. Then all at once every buffalo came up out of the water.

"What's the matter, Baldo?" asked Gulab. "What's the matter, Chando?" The two biggest buffaloes could not answer but they scrambled up the bank and came rushing toward the little boy. All the other bulls came quickly up to Gulab. Some passed him on the right side and some on the left. Quickly they made a ring around him with their backs toward him and their horns on the outside of the circle.

Then Gulab heard a snarl, a growl, and a roar. A flash of yellow leaped out of the jungle and came toward him with a great jump. It was a tiger. Gulab had heard about tigers but no tiger had been seen near their village for many years. Now he understood what had happened. The tiger had seen him playing on the bank and had decided to have him for dinner. It had been creeping quietly toward him from thicket to thicket. Gulab had not seen nor heard the tiger, but the buffaloes had smelled him and had hurried out of the pond to save the boy's life. They had made a ring around him so the tiger could not get past their horns to hurt him. But Gulab was more frightened than he had ever been in his life before. The tiger walked all around that circle of horns growling and snarling and roaring. It tried and tried to get through to the little boy. But the buffaloes stood so close together that there was no gap between their horns.

Finally Gulab decided what to do. He grabbed Baldo's tail with both hands and managed to climb up onto Baldo's back. Now he was up so high the tiger could not reach him. Then Gulab called to the buffaloes, "Open out." The buffaloes made a straight line facing the tiger. "Charge" shouted Gulab. The buffaloes charged toward the tiger with thundering hoofs and fiery nostrils. The tiger gave a great leap to one side trying to get out of their way. But the buffaloes on that side headed him off. The tiger was forced to turn and run for his life in front of the angry buffaloes. They chased him through the jungle till they came to a ravine. This was like a huge ditch which ran along the ground for many miles. The tiger leaped across and ran away growling, howling and snarling. The buffaloes could not follow the tiger any longer because they could not get across the ravine.

Then Gulab and the buffaloes went back to the village. Gulab told the people about the tiger. Some of the men went to the palace and told the Rajah about it. The Rajah was the ruler of that part of India. The Rajah was glad to hear about the tiger because six white men had come to his palace to ask him where they could find tigers to hunt. As soon as these men heard about the tiger they said that they would go to the other side of the ravine with their guns and kill the tiger. They went to the other side of the ravine and looked for the tiger. At last they saw him. They shot him and wounded him but they did not kill him. He managed to jump across the ravine again and then he hid in a dense thicket.

When the villagers heard where the tiger was they said, "Our buffaloes can drive him out of the thicket and then your men can kill him." So some of the men brought out the thirty bull buffaloes and lined them up on one side of the thicket. The six hunters got up in trees on the other side and pointed their guns at the thicket.

The villagers said to the buffaloes "Stand in line." When the buffaloes were all lined up the villagers shouted "Charge." Then the buffaloes charged right through that thicket trampling it all down. The tiger had to run out the other side. The hunters shot at the tiger again but still he did not drop dead. But now he could not run fast so the buffaloes caught up with him and trampled him to death.

The six white men started to climb down from the trees where they had been when they shot the tiger. But the villagers called quickly, "Go up the trees again. Don't let the buffaloes see you. They do not like strangers." The villagers knew that the white men would look strange to the buffaloes. So they stayed up in the trees until the buffaloes were gone. But the villagers did not take the buffaloes back to the village. They left them at the pond to cool off.

The men came down from the trees and ate their lunch. Then they decided to walk around for a while before they went back to the Rajah's palace. The tiger was dead. They thought they had nothing to fear. But they happened to walk where the buffaloes could see them from the pond. The buffaloes stood up and bellowed and then started after the white men. The men ran as fast as they could and once more climbed trees. They thought the buffaloes would soon forget about them and go back to the pond. But instead the buffaloes stood underneath the trees looking up at them, pawing the ground angrily and rattling their horns.

Toward evening Gulab went to the pond to bring the buffaloes home but no buffaloes were there. He called them but they did not come. Then he saw some of them under a tree. Gulab went over to them and saw that they were very angry. He looked up in the tree and saw one of the men. Then he saw other men in other trees with the angry buffaloes standing below.

Gulab shouted, "Down Baldo! Down Chando!" But the buffaloes were so angry they paid no attention to Gulab.

"Down," Gulab called again. "Down or I shall spank you." The buffaloes did not obey him. So Gulab rushed to Baldo and spanked him on the jaw. He rushed to Chando and spanked him on the jaw. He went from one buffalo to another spanking their jaws. Then those huge animals that had charged the tiger and terrified the hunters obeyed that little boy. They blinked and lowered their heads. Gulab climbed up by Baldo's horns and saw on his back.

"Now, turn around," shouted Gulab. The buffaloes slowly turned away from the trees and headed toward the village. Gulab called back to the men "You may come down now." Then he shouted "March" to the herd and they went peacefully back to the village.

When the hunters got back to the Rajah's palace they told him what had happened. He was very pleased with Gulab. "I must see that boy," he said. "He has made the buffaloes love him and has taught them to obey. He helped us get the tiger before it killed anyone. Now he helped the hunters get away from the buffaloes. I will invite him to come to the birthday party I am giving for my boy."

So Gulab got to visit the Rajah's palace. He got to eat cake and ice cream and candy which he had never before tasted in all his life. And he went home with presents for all his family. It was a wonderful day for Gulab and when he was a man he used to tell his children and grand children about the rewards the Rajah had given him.

The Lord Jesus Christ is greater than any Rajah or King. He is going to reward His children who do things to please Him. He wants to give us rewards so much that He is bringing them with Him when He calls us up to meet Him in the air. After He has given us our rewards He will take us to His beautiful palace.

Are we doing things that please Him? The Bible tells us how to please the Lord. The rewards the Lord will give will be far nicer than those the Rajah gave Gulab and they will last forever and ever.

NELLIE'S REWARD

"Behold I come quickly; and My reward is with Me, to give every man according as his work shall be." Revelation 22:12

(Retold from "Wilfred Gray's Text Roll," by C. J. L.;
now out of print)

"I want you to come straight home from school, girls," said Mrs. James to her two daughters, May and Nellie. They were just starting off for school with their books and lunch pails.

Nellie, the younger girl, said, "All right, Mother, we will."

But May answered crossly, "Oh, Mother, how tiresome! Charlotte wants us to go home with her after school. She is going to show us the presents her sailor uncle brought from China."

"I want you to hurry home today," answered Mrs. James. "But you may tell Charlotte that I can spare you girls after school tomorrow, if that is convenient to her mother."

"Why can't we go today?" asked May.

"I cannot give you my reason now," said Mrs. James, "but I wish you to come right home after school today. Hurry off, or you will be late."

Silently the two girls started for school. After a while May said, "I think Mother could have let us go today just as well as tomorrow. If there were any reason for it, I wouldn't care, but I believe she just likes to boss us."

"Oh, May!" said Nellie. "How can you talk that way about Mother? She does so much for us, and often she lets us do as we like. We can wait till tomorrow to see Charlotte's things. I don't think Charlotte will care. We must obey Mother even if we don't know just why she wants us to hurry home today."

"It's easy for you to obey without any reason," said May, "because you are not clever. But I always want to know the reason for everything. Miss Wilson says that is why I always get A in Science."

"I know I don't get as many A's as you do," said Nellie, sadly, but my teacher says it is because I have to be absent so much. I like to know the reason for things, too. But we have a reason for obeying Mother. The Bible says, 'Children, obey your parents in all things: for this is well pleasing unto the Lord' (Col. 3:20)."

By this time the girls were in sight of the school, and they soon joined the other pupils, each going into her own room.

As Nellie was in a lower grade, she did not see May again till lunch time. Then May ate lunch with Charlotte and walked around with her afterward, taking no notice of Nellie. When the other girls asked May and Charlotte to come and play ball, May answered, "We don't care to."

When school was out, Nellie waited for May to walk home with her. May and Charlotte came out of their room last of all. Charlotte said to Nellie, "You go on home. May is going around by my place, but she can walk faster than you, so she will get home about as soon as you do. If you should get home first, just tell your mother, 'May's coming.' "

"But Mother said we were to come straight home from school today," said Nellie. "Do come, May."

"I'm coming," said May, "but I don't want you to wait for me. Go on home."

Nellie started off slowly by herself. She could not believe May would deliberately disobey their mother, but why did she not come with her? Nellie looked back and saw May walking off with Charlotte toward her home, so she went sadly home by herself.

But the minute Nellie opened the door of her home, she forgot all about May's disobedience. There was her sailor father, who had been away many months. He had not been expected for several weeks more. "Oh, Father, it is so nice to see you!" exclaimed Nellie as she flew into his arms.

"And so my little Nellie is the first to welcome Father home," he said, as he took her in his arms. "Mother had a letter yesterday telling her that it was possible I might be home today. But I said, 'Don't tell the girls, in case I cannot get leave.' You see, I didn't want my children crying themselves to sleep, if for any reason I could not come. But where is May?"

"She's coming, Father," said Nellie. Then she listened eagerly as her father told about his adventures on the voyage. When supper was ready, May still had not come, and so the others started without her. They were nearly through eating when May come in. When she saw her father she did not rush in with a cry of joy as Nellie had. She slipped into her seat at the table looking very much ashamed of herself. Her mother did not ask any questions, as she did not want to sadden her husband's home-coming.

After the supper had been cleared away, and they had read the Bible and prayed together, Mr. James said, "I found something in a port where we called, which I think will please one of my girls. They did not have another or I would have gotten one for each of my children. Now the question is, To which girl shall I give it? I want to give it to the one who has behaved best in my absence. Which of my girls has been most obedient and has tried hardest to please her mother?"

For a minute no one spoke, then May said "Give it to Nellie.

She deserves it, and I don't. I disobeyed Mother today." Then May turned to her mother and said, "I am sorry I did not come straight home from school as you told me to. I thought I could go round by Charlotte's house and still get home as quickly as Nellie, if I ran. But Charlotte kept on showing me things and the time just flew by. I never dreamed of Father's coming today. Oh, I wish I had come straight home as you told me!" And May's eyes filled with tears.

"Your father asked me not to mention his coming, so you would not be disappointed if something hindered him," said her mother. "I think you have been punished enough already for your disobedience, so we will say no more about it."

"One of the first things a sailor has to learn is to obey orders, whether he understands the reason for them or not," said May's father as he put his arm around her.

"May is right," said Mrs. James. "The reward of obedience is Nellie's."

Nellie opened her package with fingers that trembled with joy. Inside was a beautiful Bible bound in purple velvet with gold edges and a gold clasp.

On the flyleaf of the Bible Mr. James wrote:

"Nellie James,

With love,

From her father."

"Jesus said, 'Behold, I come quickly; and my reward is with me, to give every man acording as his work shall be' (Rev. 22:12)."

That night when the girls were alone together in their room, May said, "I am not a bit jealous, Nellie. I know you really try to do what the Bible says. I am a Christian, too, but I have tried to please myself, instead of trying to please the Lord and Mother. After this, when I am tempted to disobey, I am going to remember Father's home-coming."

Trusting Jesus

Give of Your Best to the Master

Thy Word Have I Hid In My Heart

Adapted by E. O. S.

E. O. SELLERS

SUGGESTED PLAN
WHEN USING THIS COURSE FOR THIRTEEN LESSONS

First Day —   Story, "The Stolen Ring"
                 Song, "Even a Child"
                 Memory Verse, Proverbs 28:11

Second Day —   Story, "Better Than the Beach"
                 Song, "I Was Glad"
                 Memory Verse, Hebrews 10:25

Third Day —   Story, "A Wasted Birthday Present?"
                 Review above two songs
                 Memory Verse, Psalm 122:1

Fourth Day —   Story, "The Robber's Revenge"
                 Song, "The Lord Is in His Holy Temple"
                 Memory Verse, Habakkuk 2:20

Fifth Day —   Story, "Mother Doesn't Love Us Anymore"
                 Song, "Trusting Jesus"
                 Memory Verse, Proverbs 3:5

Sixth Day —   Story, "Island Prisoner," Part 1
                 Song, "Give of Your Best to the Master"
                 Memory Verse, Matthew 6:24

Seventh Day — Story, "Island Prisoner," Part 2
                 Song, "Read Your Bible"
                 Memory Verse, Isaiah 34:16

Eighth Day —   Story, "Island Prisoner," Part 3
                 Song, "Thy Word Have I Hid in My Heart"
                 Memory Verse, Psalm 119:11

Ninth Day —   Story, "The Broken Window"
                 Review Songs
                 Review Verses

Tenth Day —   Story, "That Old Red Sweater"
                 Review Songs
                 Memory Verse, James 1:22

Eleventh Day - Story, "Gulab and the Tiger Hunt"
                 Song, "Jesus Christ is Coming for Me?"
                 Memory Verse, Revelation 22:12

Twelfth Day -   Story, "Nellie's Reward"
                 Review Songs
                 Review Verses
                 Let children dramatize one of the stories, which they can use in a program for their parents.

Thirteenth Day: Present program suggested on next page.

Note: A series of ten texts to color 8½ x 11 in., each containing all or part of the words of one of the verses taught through these stories is available and can be used before or after the session to help fix the memory verses in the child's mind. There is an eleventh sheet to color in the pack, which is to be used as a cover if the texts are to be made into a Wild Flower Booklet.

62

All sing "Even a Child"
One child recites Proverbs 28:11. All recite it in unison.
One child recites Hebrews 10:25. All recite it in unison.
All sing "I Was Glad. "
One child recites Psalm 122:1. All recite it in unison.
One child recites Habakkuk 2:20. All recite it in unison.
All sing "The Lord Is in His Holy Temple."
One child recites Proverbs 3:5. All recite it in unison.
All sing "Trusting Jesus."
One child recites Matthew 6:24. All recite it in unison.
All sing "Give of Your Best to the Master."
One child recites Isaiah 34:16. All recite it in unison.
All sing "Read Your Bible."
One Child recites Psalm 119:11. All recite it in unison.
All sing "Thy Word Have I Hid in My Heart."
One child recites James 1:22. All recite it in unison.
Present dramatized story.
One child recites Revelation 22:12. All recite it in unison.
All sing "Jesus Christ is Coming for Me."

"CONDUCT TOWARD GOD"

1. Does God notice how children behave?
"Even a child is known by his doings, whether his work be pure, and whether it be right." Proverbs 20:11.

2. Should we keep on going to Sunday School?
"Not forsaking the assembling of ourselves together, as the manner of some is." Hebrews 10:25.

3. What did David say when he was invited to God's house?
"I was glad when they said unto me, Let us go into the house of the Lord." Psalm 122:1.

4. Should we be quiet in Sunday School?
"The Lord is in His holy temple; let all the earth keep silence before him." Habakkuk 2:20.

5. Should we trust in the Lord?
"Trust in the Lord with all thine heart; and lean not unto thine own understanding." Proverbs 3:5.

6. Can we serve God and Satan both?
"No man can serve two masters." Matthew 6:24.

7. Should we read the Bible?
"Seek ye out of the book of the Lord, and read." Isaiah 34:16.

8. Why should we memorize God's Word?
"Thy word have I hid in mine heart, that I might not sin against Thee." Psalm 119:11.

9. What should we do after we know God's word?
"Be ye doers of the word, and not hearers only, deceiving your own selves." James 1:22.

10. Will the Lord reward those who try to please him?
"Behold, I come quickly; and My reward is with Me, to give every man according as his work shall be." Revelation 22:12.